BILLY AND THE MINI MONSTERS

MONSTERS GO TO A PARTY!

Illustrated by
ZANNA DAVIDSON • MELANIE WILLIAMSON

Meet Billy...

Billy was just
an ordinary boy
living an ordinary
life, until
ONE NIGHT
he found
five
**MINI
MONSTERS**
in his sock drawer.

Gloop   Peep   Fang-Face   Captain Snott   Trumpet

Then he saved their lives, and they swore never to leave him.

We give you the Secret-Hairy-Snot-Tooth Oath of Devotion.

We're awesome!

And fun!

And SCARY!

Are we scary? I'm not sure I'm very scary.

One thing was certain – Billy's life would never be the same **AGAIN**...

Contents

Party!

Chapter 1
Party Time

Billy was
very excited.
It was his friend
Jack's birthday,
and he was going to
his dressing-up party.

Unfortunately, his little sister Ruby was friends with Jack's little sister, so she was coming too.

But Billy found it very HARD to
be nice to Ruby.

She destroyed
his toys...

...ruined his games...

…and always wanted to play in his bedroom.

There was **NO WAY** Billy was going to let Ruby into his bedroom.

Ruby had to learn that Billy's bedroom was PRIVATE.

Because Billy had his
TOP SECRET
pets to protect.

The MINI MONSTERS!

"We can't wait to come to the party!" said Captain Snott. "I've been practising the birthday song."

The Mini Monsters had been busy dreaming about Jack's birthday party **ALL WEEK**.

"I'm sorry but you can't come to the party," said Billy. "Not after what's happened the last few times."

The Mini Monsters were always getting into trouble:

At the swimming pool...

Fang-Face and Captain Snott nearly drowning.

Gloop being SUCKED down the drain.

At home...

All of the monsters getting trapped in the washing machine.

At school...

Peep ending up in
a hamster cage... →

...and Trumpet sinking in
a vat of baked beans.

And at the airport...

Gloop and Trumpet getting
lost with the luggage.

Billy had caused so much trouble trying to rescue them he'd had **NO TV FOR A WEEK.**

Billy knew if the Mini Monsters came to the party, he would end up in **EVEN MORE** trouble.

"I'll make it up to you," said Billy.
"I'll bring you back some cake!"

I want you to stay RIGHT here.

We promise.

"Bye," called Billy. And he went out of his room, and shut the door.

16

Up you come.

Let's go!

17

At the party...

Just remember - we have to stick together.

Chapter 2
The Magic Show

Billy sat down with his friends.
There was going to be a magic show.

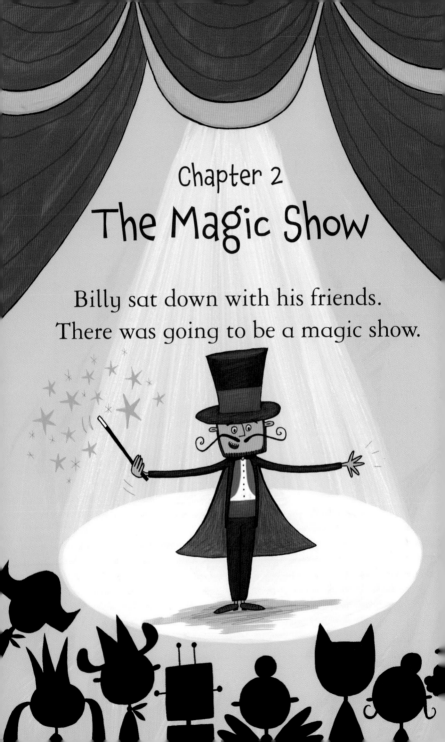

"Let the show **begin**!"
said the magician.

He magicked
FLAMES
from his
wand…

…made amazing
balloon animals…

…and even sawed the birthday boy in half.

"And now for my final and favourite trick — the rabbit in the hat!" the magician said.

The magician tapped his hat
three times…

one

two

three

Then he put his
hand **inside**…

and pulled out…

23

26

Chapter 3
Up and Away

Billy *rushed* over to the magician. He had to get Fang-Face back. But Jack's mum was making everyone go outside.

Time for the treasure hunt in the garden.

There was nothing Billy could do. But then, outside, he saw…

He had to rescue them.
What if they were…

…eaten by a bird…

…or **swept** out to sea…

…or carried into

OUTER SPACE?

Billy tried catching the balloon, but he couldn't jump high enough.

He tried spearing
the balloon with a
stick…

He **missed**.

"This isn't good," thought Billy.
Then the wind started to blow
harder. He ran this way…

…and that way, chasing the
balloon across the garden. But the
balloon kept slipping from his grasp.

33

The balloon was heading over the garden wall… but, at the last moment, its string caught in a tree. "Phew!" said Billy.

A very

tall

tree.

"Oh no!" said Billy as he looked up. There was only one thing for it.

He took a deep breath and began to climb.

By now, a small crowd had gathered beneath him.

"Go on, Billy!" cried Jack.

No one's ever made it to the top of that tree before.

Careful, Billy!

Billy kept on climbing. Even though the branches were getting very thin...

35

He reached across for the Mini Monsters.

That was fun!

Shall we do it again?

The branch creaked and swayed in the wind. Billy wondered if he was going to **FALL**. Slowly, carefully, he picked up the Mini Monsters.

By the time Billy got back down, his legs felt all **wobbly**.

Ruby was watching him very closely. "What's in your hand?" she asked.

"Well, I've got a SECRET too," said Ruby. "It's small and hairy, but really amazing. I'll tell you mine if you tell me yours."

Normally, Billy wasn't interested in Ruby's secrets, but when she said **SMALL AND HAIRY**, he couldn't help wondering if Ruby HAD found a Mini Monster? Were they *all* at the party?

"Okay," he said at last. "Tell me yours first."

I've found a little pink hamster. **WITH WINGS.**

Where is it?

Not telling...

...until you tell me YOUR secret.

Ruby's secret sounded a lot like
Peep. Billy *had* to get him back.

"This is a very important secret,"
said Billy. "Here goes."

40

41

42

43

Chapter 4
Peep the Doll

"Wow!" said Ruby, when Billy had finished telling her his secret.

"You've got little pet monsters that are **ALIVE!**

Can I meet them?"

Billy looked around to make sure no one was watching.

Then he OPENED his hand…

"WOW!" said Ruby again, and she bent down to give Captain Snott a kiss.

He blushed.

Then she patted Trumpet on the head.

"And there are *more* of them?" Ruby asked excitedly.

Billy nodded. "I need your help finding them. This is what they look like…" He took out a pencil and some paper.

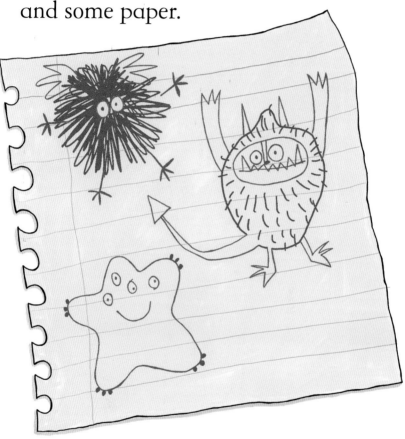

"Ooh!" said Ruby. "The hairy one's my hamster! Follow me!"

"Remember," said Billy, as they went into the house.

No one must realize what we're up to.

We're a team!

Together, they CREPT UPSTAIRS...

ALONG THE CORRIDOR...

And into Jack's sister's room.

"In there," whispered Ruby. "In the dolls' house."

Hello, Peep!

"Quick!" Ruby
called through the door.
"Someone's coming."

50

Billy just had time to slip the
Mini Monsters into his cape pocket,
when Jack's mum came
into the room.

What are
you doing
in here?

"I was just showing Billy the
dolls' house," said Ruby. "Billy
loves dolls' houses."

Billy nodded.

Jack's mum looked **SUSPICIOUS**.

"Well, come downstairs," she said. "It's nearly time for tea."

"I think we're in trouble," whispered Ruby as they walked down.

You should be with the rest of the party!

Billy looked at the tea table and groaned. "And I think it's about to get worse…"

54

55

My friend!

Chapter 5
Jelly and Cake

"Oh no!" thought Billy.

He could see Gloop on the tea table

pretending

to be a

jelly.

He was very good at it.

So good, that if he wasn't careful, someone was going to **EAT HIM**.

But before Billy could grab Gloop, all the other kids started coming in for tea.

Just then, Jack came forward. He was headed for

THE JELLY.

Billy leaned over to pick up Gloop… but Gloop wouldn't let go of the jelly.

Jack reached for the plate… so Billy picked up the whole jelly.

Billy was trying to move Gloop, but nothing was working.

"**Billy**," said Jack's mum again. "I asked you to put that jelly back."

Gloop! That's not another monster. It's food.

I don't believe you.

Jack's mum picked up a big spoon.
"Oh no!" thought Billy. "She's
going to **CUT** Gloop in half!"

"I'll have it," said Ruby. She
grabbed hold of Gloop and a large
lump of jelly, and put them both on
her plate.

Where are your manners?

"I'm going to have to tell
your mother about this…"

Billy looked round and realized the parents were already starting to arrive. And there was his mum, coming into the dining room.

Luckily, just then, Jack's dad called, "Get ready for the cake."

Everyone stopped looking at the jelly and started singing "Happy Birthday", except for Captain Snott.

Billy could hear his little voice piping up from inside his cape.

All the children leaned forward
to watch Jack blow out the candles.
Jack took a deep breath and...

65

Jack's mum **fainted**.
The parents screamed.

In all the confusion, Billy grabbed Fang-Face and Gloop stuffed them both inside his cape.

"That's all of them," Billy whispered to Ruby.

Party's over.

On the way home...

I love birthday parties.

Why wouldn't that monster talk to me?

68

69

70

Chapter 6
A Monster Party

When Billy and Ruby got home, their mum **marched** them into the house.

"We're sorry, Mum," said Billy, "but the good news," he added, grinning, "is that Ruby and I are now **BEST FRIENDS**."

73

74

As soon as they got upstairs,
Billy shut his bedroom door.

"Thanks for all your help today,
Ruby," he said. "Maybe little
sisters aren't so bad after all."

Ruby grinned.

"There's something we've got to
do…" Billy whispered.

"Happy birthday!" said Billy. "Thank you for being such a brilliant pet monster."

I promise never to call you a hamster again.

"Then it really is my BEST birthday ever," said Peep.

All about the
MINI MONSTERS

FANG-FACE →

LIKES EATING:
socks, school ties,
paper, or anything
that comes his way.

SPECIAL SKILL:
has massive fangs.

**SCARE FACTOR:
9/10**

← GLOOP

LIKES EATING: cake.

SPECIAL SKILL:
very stre-e-e-e-tchy.
Gloop can also swallow
his own eyeballs and
make them reappear on
any part of his body.

**SCARE FACTOR:
4/10**

CAPTAIN SNOTT

LIKES EATING: bogeys.

SPECIAL SKILL:
can glow in the dark.

SCARE
FACTOR:
5/10

PEEP

LIKES EATING: very small flies.

SPECIAL SKILL: can fly (but
not very far, or very well).

SCARE FACTOR:
0/10 (unless you're afraid of
small hairy things)

TRUMPET

LIKES EATING: cheese.

SPECIAL SKILL:
amazingly powerful
cheese-powered parps.

SCARE FACTOR:
7/10
(taking into
account his parps)

Designed by Brenda Cole
Edited by Becky Walker
Cover design by Hannah Cobley
Digital manipulation by John Russell

This edition first published in 2020 by Usborne Publishing Ltd.,
Usborne House, 83-85 Saffron Hill, London EC1N 8RT, England.
Usborne.com Copyright © 2020, 2017 Usborne Publishing Ltd.